# "Take Care of Things," Edward Said

To Davie Gracey, friend of children—H.E.B.

To Adam, who Takes Care of Booger, Thunder, and Frisbee—K.C.

Library of Congress Cataloging in Publication Data. Buckley, Helen Elizabeth. "Take care of things," Edward said / Helen E. Buckley ; pictures by Katherine Coville.    p.    cm. Summary: Going off to school, Edward tells his brother Tom to take care of things, so Tom takes care of the swings, bikes, toys, cat, and dogs by treating them all as his brother would want them treated. ISBN 0-688-07731-5 : ISBN 0-688-07732-3 (lib. bdg.) : [1. Brothers—Fiction.]  I. Coville, Katherine, ill.  II. Title.  PZ7.B882Tak 1991  [E]—dc19   88-1578 CIP·AC

# Helen E. Buckley

# "Take Care of Things," Edward Said

illustrated by Katherine Coville

Lothrop, Lee & Shepard Books    New York

Summer was over
and Tom's brother, Edward,
was going back to school.
Tom went down the path with him
to wait for the school bus.

King, Cass, and Kitterly
ran along beside them.
When the bus came,
Tom wanted to shout,
"Don't go, Edward! Don't go to school!"
Edward climbed onto the bus
and waved to Tom.

"Take care of things," Edward called.
The bus pulled away.
Tom went up the path to the house.
King, Cass, and Kitterly followed him.

"Edward's gone to school," he told them.
They sat down on the steps.
"Edward will be home
before you know it," said Mom.
"Hang in there," said Dad.
They kissed Tom good-bye
and went off to work.

Tom looked at the swings
hanging empty from the tree.

He looked at the bikes
standing empty by the garage.
He remembered what Edward had said:
"Take care of things."

"Want to swing, swings?" Tom asked.
He sat in each one
and swung himself back and forth.

"Want to go for a ride, bikes?"
Tom rode his bike down the path and back.
Edward's bike was too big for him to ride,
so he walked it.

Tom went into the house.
Mrs. Henderson was watering the plants.
"Hi, Tom," she said.
"What are you going to do today?"
"I'm taking care of things," Tom said.
"Good," said Mrs. Henderson.
"Kitterly's dish is empty,
and King and Cass need water."

Tom filled the dishes with water and food.
King, Cass, and Kitterly watched him.
"I'm taking care of you," he told them.

Tom went down the hall to Edward's room
and looked in the turtle box.
"Edward will be home before you know it,"
he told the turtles.

He looked at all the toy animals
on Edward's shelf.
"Want to have a parade?" he asked.
He lined them up around the room.

Mrs. Henderson came in to make Edward's bed.
"See my parade?" Tom said.
"I certainly do," said Mrs. Henderson.
"Don't you think that fine parade
should have some music?"

Tom took Edward's drum down from the shelf and played as he marched around the room. Mrs. Henderson marched back to the kitchen.

Tom took some blocks from the toy box.
"Now I'll make a bridge for you to walk over,"
he told the animals.

Pretty soon Mrs. Henderson called him to lunch.
Chicken noodle soup was Tom's favorite,
but today he didn't finish his soup.

"What's the matter, Tom?" Mrs. Henderson asked.
"I didn't do what Edward said today," said Tom.
"I didn't take care of things."

Mrs. Henderson put her arm around him.
"Didn't you swing the swings
and ride the bikes and feed
King, Cass, and Kitterly?"
"Yes," said Tom. "But then I just played."

"I heard you talking to the turtles,"
said Mrs. Henderson.
"And didn't you have a parade for the animals
and make them a bridge?
And didn't you play Edward's drum?"

"Is that taking care of things?" Tom asked.
"It certainly is!" said Mrs. Henderson.
"That's exactly what pets and toys need—
to be talked to and played with.
Edward will say you did a fine job."

"He will?"
"Of course he will!
Now let's put everything away
and then it will be nap time.
And then Edward will be home."

Tom lay down on Edward's bed.
Kitterly curled up beside him.
King and Cass stretched out on the rug.
Before he knew it,
Mrs. Henderson was at the door.
"Wake up, Tom. It's time for the bus."

Tom and Kitterly jumped off the bed,
King and Cass leaped up,
and they all ran out of the room,
out of the house,
and down the path to the road.

The bus came to a stop.
The big door opened,
and there was Edward!
"Hi, Tom, I'm home!" Edward said.

As the bus pulled away,
they started up the path to the house.
"What did you do all day?" Edward asked.
"I took care of things," Tom said.
"Good," said Edward. "I knew you would."